No Cook Cook Book

For Smt. Deepika Sen, with all my love

Published in 2006 by

Rupa . Co

7/16, Ansari Road, Daryaganj,
New Delhi 110002

Sales Centres:
Allahabad Bangalore Chandigarh Chennai
Hyderabad Jaipur Kathmandu
Kolkata Mumbai Pune

Cover & Book Design by
Kapil Gupta
kapilkgupta@hotmail.com

Printed in India by
Gopsons Papers Ltd.
A-14 Sector 60
Noida 201 301

No Cook Cook Book

Satarupa Banerjee

Rupa & Co

Foreword

Dear fellow food lovers, do you, like me, loathe at times to labour over a hot stove to cook a meal? There can be so many reasons–maybe you don't have time, or you simply like food that's not overcooked and offers the maximum amount of goodness; or you're feeling out of sorts; or you're just plain lazy.

Whatever the reason, give yourself a holiday from cooking, as you rush around doing your everyday chores. Rustle up a simple no-cook meal–an appetiser to begin with, followed by a cold soup and a sandwich; then a chilled dessert. From breakfast to dinner, you can avoid cooking, yet have (in fact, enjoy) interesting and satisfying meals.

Follow this fire-free repertoire of dishes that not only do not require cooking, but tickle the taste buds. Nothing could be simpler and more 'clean', to prepare and taste. At the most, in some cases you may have to do a bit of boiling.

Quite obviously, when eating food raw or uncooked, it is essential you choose products that are fresh and of excellent quality. So, invest in top quality ingredients and you will be rewarded with extra flavour and nutritional benefits.

With the interesting new ideas that this book offers, I wish you may enjoyable no-cook meals.

Coffee Eggnog

Ideal liquid breakfast

- 2 eggs, white and yolk separated
- $^{1}/_{3}$ cup powdered sugar, or to taste
- 2 tbsp instant coffee powder
- a dash of salt
- 1 tsp vanilla essence
- 2 cups milk, chilled
- ¾ cup water
- 1 cup whipped cream
- 2 tsp chocolate chips

In a small bowl, beat the egg whites until soft peaks form. Gradually beat in the sugar until stiff once more.

In a large bowl, beat the egg yolks until lemon coloured. Slowly, beat in the coffee powder, salt, vanilla essence, milk and water.

Stir in the beaten egg whites and whipped cream. Mix well.

Serve chilled in two stem glasses, decorated with chocolate chips.

Serves 2

Note: If chocolate chips are not available, shave a bar of milk chocolate and use.

Meal In A Glass

If you don't have the time to cook breakfast, here's the answer.

1 cup curd

1 large banana, pureed

2 tbsp powdered sugar or to taste

2 tbsp chopped nuts and a few slices of banana for decoration

Mix well the curd, pureed banana, and sugar in a blender till smooth. Chill.

Serve in tall glasses with crushed ice. If you desire you can thin down the drink with a little milk or water.

Garnish with chopped nuts and slices of banana.

Serves 2

Note: If you are not fond of bananas, any other fruit or a combination of fruits may be used like mango, chickoo, custard apple, honeydew melon.

Nutritious Chocolate Shake

Wonderful as a complete protein breakfast drink or as an any-time snack. Wheat germ is available in health food shops.

3 cups milk
1 cup homemade paneer, well drained
1 large, ripe mango, diced
4 tbsp drinking chocolate powder
2 tbsp honey
1 tbsp wheat germ
a dash of nutmeg powder

Mix all the ingredients in a blender. Blend until smooth and creamy. Chill.

Pour into tall glasses. Sprinkle the nutmeg and serve.

Serves 4

Note: Any fresh fruit in season like custard apple, chickoo, banana, papaya or strawberries can be substituted for mango.

Iced Tomato Cooler

A perfect treat for hot summer months.

½ kg red ripe tomatoes
1 small onion, chopped
1 tsp sugar
½ tsp salt
1 cup thin cream, chilled
1 tbsp finely chopped fresh coriander

Blend the tomatoes and onion together to a puree.

Strain and add sugar and salt. Chill.

Add the chilled cream and blend well.

Taste and adjust seasonings. Stir in fresh coriander.

Serve chilled in mugs garnished with lemon slices.

Serves 4

Gazpacho

A classic Spanish soup, cold Gazpacho makes a refreshing summer lunch served with small bowls of chopped olives, cucumber, capsicum and onion.

4 large ripe red tomatoes, chopped
2 cloves of garlic, chopped
1 medium cucumber, diced
1 medium capsicum, chopped
2 slices of bread, soaked in water and squeezed
1 tbsp chopped parsley
2 tbsp refined oil
1 tbsp vinegar
1 tsp sugar
a pinch of chilli powder
1 tsp salt
½ tsp black pepper powder
4 ice cubes

Put the tomatoes, garlic, cucumber, capsicum, bread, parsley, oil and vinegar in a blender and blend to a puree. Strain. Stir in the sugar, chilli powder, salt and pepper.

Add the ice cubes and chill. The ice, as it melts, makes the soup creamy in consistency.

Garnish with a little cream if desired before serving.

Pass extra bowls of finely diced onion, cucumber and capsicum. Each person can sprinkle his or her own soup with a little of these accompaniments according to individual tastes.

Serves 4

Lebanese Cucumber Soup

This traditional summer soup is enjoyed throughout the Middle East. There are many variations of the recipe.

6 tbsp raisins
2 small cucumbers
1½ cups thick fresh curd
1 cup full-cream milk
4 tbsp chopped walnuts
½ tsp salt or to taste
¼ tsp white pepper powder or to taste
6 ice cubes
2 tbsp finely chopped mint

Soak the raisins in hot water for 15 minutes.

Peel and grate the cucumbers.

Place the curd in a large bowl. Add the milk and 1 cup of iced water. Blend with a hand-held electric beater or whisk till thoroughly blended.

Drain the raisins and add to the curd mixture along with the walnuts, salt, pepper and cucumber.

Stir in the ice cubes. Cover and chill for 2–3 hours.

Serve in small bowls, garnished with mint.

Serves 4

Chilled Avocado Soup

Exotic vegetables and fruits are easily available in our markets these days. So why not make the best of them?

- 2 ripe avocados
- 1 tbsp lime juice
- 4 cups milk
- ½ tsp salt
- ½ tsp pepper
- 2 tbsp chopped fresh coriander
- 6 tbsp cream.

Cut the avocados in half and then twist the two halves apart. Remove the stone, peel the skin and dice the flesh.

Blend the avocado flesh along with the lime juice and milk till smooth.

Season with salt and pepper and refrigerate.

Serve chilled garnished with fresh coriander.

Serves 2

Chicken and Rice Ring

Filling and delicious. Very easy to prepare too!

1 cup mayonnaise
2 tbsp finely chopped onion
1 tbsp chopped fresh coriander
1 tbsp chopped mint
½ tsp salt
½ tsp black pepper powder
1 cup cooked rice
1 tomato diced
1 capsicum chopped
4 tbsp cooked corn
2 cups cooked, flaked chicken
5 pineapple slices, diced
or
1 cup grapes
2 rings pineapple and 15 grapes for garnishing.

Mix the mayonnaise, onion, fresh coriander, mint, salt and tsp pepper. Divide into two portions.

To one part of the mayonnaise mix, add the cooked rice, tomato, capsicum and corn.

Grease a ring mould and place the rice mixture in it. Press firmly. Chill for 2 hours.

In the meantime, mix the chicken, pineapple or grapes and the remaining mayonnaise mix. Chill.

Unmould the rice onto a serving platter. Fill the centre with the chicken mixture.

Garnish with the pineapple and grapes and serve.

Serves 4

Curd Rice

A perfect dish for our scorching tropical heat.

4 cups slightly overcooked rice
1½ cups curd
½ cup cream
½ cup milk
½ tsp salt or to taste
1 tbsp sugar
1 small cucumber, peeled and finely chopped
1 tomato, chopped fine
a handful of chopped coriander leaves
1 green chilli, chopped
½ cup grated carrots
$^1/_3$ red pomegranate seeds

Mash the rice a little.

Blend together the curd, cream, milk, sugar and salt. Stir the rice into the curd. Mix well.

Pour on a rice plate. Garnish with the cucumber, tomato, carrot, coriander leaves and green chillies.

Top this with the pomegranate seeds and serve at room temperature. All that is needed to complete the meal is a pickle.

Serves 4

Cucumber Cheese Mousse

A delicious, though slightly uncommon treat.

Juice of 1 lemon
1 tbsp gelatine
$1^1/_3$ cups water
1 tbsp powdered sugar
1 large cucumber, peeled and diced
$^2/_3$ cup mayonnaise
½ cup hung curd
½ cup whipped cream
1 tsp salt
1 tsp pepper
1 tbsp chopped dill or parsley
½ cup mayonnaise
8 cucumber slices
8 tomato slices and lettuce leaves for
garnishing.

Combine the lime juice, water and sugar. Soak the gelatine in it for 15 minutes. Dissolve gelatine over hot water. Cool to room temperature.

Blend $^2/_3$ cup mayonnaise, curd and cream well. Mix the cucumber and dill with the mayonnaise mixture. Gradually beat in the cooled gelatine, salt and pepper.

Spoon into an oiled circular mould. Chill till set. Unmould onto a serving dish.

Garnish with the cucumber, tomato & lettuce leaves. Pass ½ cup mayonnaise on the side.

Serves 4

Note: You can use lime crystal jelly instead of gelatine.

Savory Prawn Cheesecake

Cheesecakes can be savory, too. This is a glamorous cheesecake –perfect buffet food and makes an exciting addition to your no-cooking repertoire.

Base: ½ cup butter, melted
24 cream cracker biscuits, ground into crumbs
3 tbsp chopped fresh parsley or coriander
¼ tsp salt.
1 tsp pepper.
Filling: 2 tbsp gelatine
6 tbsp water
450 gm paneer
¼ cup milk
grated rind of 1 lime
2 tbsp lime juice
4 eggs, separated into white and yolk
1 tbsp tomato puree
1 cup cream
1 tsp salt
½ tsp pepper
½ cup cooked prawns
Topping: 175 gm paneer
3 tbsp mayonnaise
4 tbsp chopped fresh parsley or coriander
1 tsp lime juice
8 prawns for garnishing.

Grease a loose bottomed flat tin 10"–12" (25 cm–30 cm) in diameter.

Base: Mix the melted butter with the biscuit crumbs, parsley, salt and pepper. Spread the mixture into the prepared tin and press evenly all over the base. Refrigerate till ready to use.

Filling: Soak the gelatine in the water for 5 minutes. Dissolve over hot water. Set aside.

Blend the paneer with the milk in a Mixer till smooth. Blend in the lime rind and juice, egg yolks, tomato puree and cream.

Stir in the dissolved gelatine, salt and pepper. Chill until slightly thickened.

In the meantime, whisk the egg whites until stiff. Fold lightly but thoroughly into the chilled paneer mixture along with the prawns.

Pour into the prepared tin. Level surface. Chill until set, about 3–4 hours.

Run a knife around the sides of the set cheesecake. Remove from the tin onto a plate.

Topping: Blend the paneer till smooth. Mix in the mayonnaise, parsley and lime juice.

Decorate the cheesecake with the paneer mixture. Garnish with prawns.

Long Island Cheesecake

An easy to assemble cheesecake.

1 pkt salted biscuits
2 tbsp butter, melted
9 cubes (225 gm) cheese, grated
225 gm paneer, grated
½ cup cream or malai
2 thick slices ham or chicken salami, finely chopped
2-3 spring onions, finely chopped
3 tbsp roasted peanuts, coarsely crushed
½ tsp salt
1 tsp pepper

Crush the biscuit and mix with the salted butter. Press onto the base of an 18 cm loose bottomed flat tin.

Blend together the cheese and paneer till smooth. Whip the cream and fold in.

Stir in half the peanuts along with salt and pepper. Add the ham or salami and spring onion.

Spread the mixture over the biscuit base and chill till set.

Remove the cheesecake from the tin and place on a serving plate. Garnish with the remaining peanuts.

Serves 6-8

Full Meal Pasta Salad

This delicious salad makes a meal by itself.

100 gm cooked small pasta like farfalle or elbow macaroni
1 small apple, unpeeled, cored and diced
10 green grapes
10 black grapes
2 celery sticks, sliced
¾ cup paneer, cubed
½ cup almonds, blanched and sliced
½ cup cream
2 tbsp mayonnaise or hung curd
¾ tsp salt
½ tsp pepper
1 cup chopped lettuce or cabbage

Place the pasta, apple, grapes, almond, celery and paneer in a bowl.

Whip the cream until thick and fold in the mayonnaise or curd. Add salt and pepper.

Stir into the pasta mixture and mix well.

Arrange the lettuce or cabbage leaves in a salad bowl and spoon the salad on top.

Serves 4

Note: You may use half cheese and half paneer and substitute almonds with cashewnuts. Cooked rice can also be used in stead of pasta.

Come to Lunch Salad

Cool and pretty, this salad will make a special summer meal.

2 cups cooked rice

2 cups cooked prawns

1 cup celery, sliced thin

$^{2}/_{3}$ cup julienned capsicum

6 rings canned pineapple, chopped

cooked prawns for garnishing

Dressing: 2 tbsp vinegar

1 tbsp lime juice

1½ tbsp refined oil or salad oil

1 tsp Worcestershire sauce

1 tsp sugar

½ tsp salt

½ tsp curry powder

$^{1}/_{8}$ tsp dry ginger powder

$^{1}/_{8}$ tsp pepper

Combine the rice, shrimp, celery, capsicum (preferably a combination of red and green) and pineapple.

Combine all the dressing ingredients in a screw-topped jar and shake well.

Pour over the rice mixture and stir. Chill and marinate at least 3 hours.

Serve garnished with more prawns.

Serves 4

Elegant Chicken Salad

The coconut seller will get you a green coconut (dab) with thick tender meat inside. Combine it with chicken for this delicious salad.

3 cups cooked chicken, cubed
1 cup diced celery
½ cup blanched, sliced almonds or broken cashewnuts
½ cup pineapple cubes
½ cup grapes, halved
½ cup diced flesh of green coconut
6 crisp lettuce leaves
Dressing: 2 tbsp finely chopped candied ginger
¼ cup chopped cashewnuts
1 tsp honey
1 cup creme fraiche (see recipe below)

Toss all the salad ingredients together except lettuce leaves. Chill. Mix all the dressing ingredients together. While serving gently fold the dressing thoroughly into the salad.

Serve in lettuce cups.

Creme fraiche
3 cups cream
2 tbsp curd

This has a lighter, fresher, more tangy flavour than ordinary cream.

Warm the cream very slightly like we do to set curd. Stir in the curd thoroughly.

Cover and leave in a warm place to set, preferably overnight. It should thicken considerably. Refrigerate. Will stay fresh in the refrigerator for 3–4 days.

Serves 6

Easy Pasta Fruit Salad

An adaptation of a Finnish recipe that can be served as a side dish or as an unusual dessert.

2 cups cooked small pasta such as shell or elbow macaroni
¼ cup walnuts, chopped
1 banana, sliced
½ cup pineapple cubes
1 orange, peeled and segmented
1 apple, cored and diced
6 lettuce leaves
12 cherries
Orange Cream Dressing: ½ cup orange juice
1 tsp lime juice
$^1/_3$ cup powdered sugar
¾ cup cream

Combine pasta, walnut, banana, pineapple, orange and apple

Divide into 6 portions and place each on a lettuce leaf. Top each portion with a little dressing.

Serve chilled, garnished with 2 cherries each.

Dressing: Whip the cream with the sugar till thick. Mix in the lime juice. Chill till needed.

Serves 6

Capsicum Rings

A colourful addition to your buffet table.

- 2 red capsicums
- 2 green capsicums
- 1 cup homemade paneer (devoid of whey)
- ½ cup hung curd
- ½ cup whipped cream
- 1 small onion, finely chopped
- ½ cup deseeded and finely chopped cucumber
- 1 tbsp deseeded and finely chopped tomatoes
- 2 green chillies, finely chopped
- 1 tsp pepper
- 1 tbsp chopped fresh coriander
- 2 cups shredded lettuce
- a handful of grapes

Cut away a thin slice from the stalk end of the capsicums and discard. Remove the seeds and pith carefully and wash. Keep inverted.

Blend well the paneer and curd. Stir in the onion, cucumber, salt, pepper and parsley. Finally, fold in the whipped cream.

Stuff the capsicums with the seasoned paneer mixture, pressing down firmly. Let them stand on a plate. Chill for at least 2 hours, longer if possible.

Serve cut into slices on a bed of shredded lettuce. Garnish with grapes.

Serves 6

Excellent Fruit Salad Dressing

- 1 cup cream, chilled
- ½ cup brown sugar
- ¼ cup vinegar
- ½ cup granulated sugar
- ½ tsp salt

Beat the cream until slightly thickened.

Add the remaining ingredients and mix well.

Refrigerate overnight to thicken.

Can be used for any salad with fruits.

Makes 1½ cups

Tomato Ring Salad

For hot days, salads can be more than just an accompaniment with the main meal. This moulded tomato ring gives salad the place it deserves on the dining table.

¾ cup water
1 tbsp gelatine
2½ cup tomato juice (about 8 large tomatoes will yield this amount)
1 tsp Worcestershire sauce
1 tsp lime juice
1 tsp salt
1 tbsp powdered sugar
1 tsp pepper
4 cubes of cheese, diced
1 small cucumber, peeled and diced
2 thick slices ham, cubed
½ cup cream, whipped
2 tbsp mayonnaise
¼ tsp curry powder
½ tsp mustard powder
fresh coriander sprigs for garnishing

Place water in a bowl and sprinkle gelatine. Heat very gently until dissolved. Cool and mix with the tomato juice, Worcestershire sauce, lime juice, sugar, salt and pepper.

Pour into a damp ring mould and refrigerate to set.

Place the cheese, cucumber and ham in a bowl. Stir in the cream, mayonnaise, curry powder and mustard. Mix well. Add salt and pepper.

Unmould the tomato ring on a plate. Spoon the cheese mixture into the centre and around the edges.

Garnish with fresh coriander sprigs and serve.

Serves 4-6

Popcorn Salad

A most unusual combination. Makes a very good snack.

6 cups popcorn
½ cup spring onion sliced
1 cup celery, diced
¾ cup mayonnaise
¾ cup chopped ham
1 cup grated cheese
½ cup sliced water chestnuts

Combine in a bowl the popcorn, onion, celery, mayonnaise, ½ cup ham, ¾ cup cheese, and water chestnuts.
Top with the remaining ham and cheese and serve at once.

Serves 6

Note: This must be served immediately; otherwise the popcorn will lose its crunch.

Mayonnaise

A wonderful easy-to-make sandwich spread and salad dressing.

2 egg yolks
1 tbsp lime juice
1 cup salad oil or refined oil
1 tsp white vinegar
½ tsp mustard powder
1½ tsp salt
½ tsp pepper
1 tsp sugar

Beat well the egg yolk in a bowl. Add the lime juice and whisk till creamy.

Add the oil drop by drop, beating all the time. Gradually increase the quantity of the oil as the mayonnaise thickens.

Halfway through, add the vinegar, mustard power, pepper and sugar

When half the oil has been absorbed by the mixture, add the remaining oil, 1 tsp at a time. It is most important to beat steadily throughout the whole process. Keep covered in the refrigerator.

You may thin down the mayonnaise with ¼ cup milk or cream while using.

Makes about 1½ cups

Frosted Sandwich Treat

A wholesome sandwich which is a meal by itself.

1 unsliced loaf of sandwich bread

½ cup butter, softened

Ham filling: 4 thick slices ham

¼ cup chopped parsley

2 tbsp mayonnaise

Pineapple filling: 1 cup finely chopped pineapple

¼ cup whipped cream

¼ cup grated cheese

¼ cup finely chopped cashewnuts or peanuts

¼ tsp salt

¼ tsp pepper

Prawn filling: 1 cup chopped cooked prawns

2 tbsp finely chopped celery

1 tbsp sweet chilli sauce

1 hardboiled egg, washed

¼ tsp salt,

pinch pepper

Frosting: 2 cups thick hung curd

½ tsp salt

½ tsp pepper

1 tbsp powdered sugar

6 cherries

6 black grapes

6 green grapes

Trim crusts from the loaf. Cut the loaf into 4 equal slices lengthwise, slightly flatten each with a rolling pin.

Spread 1 side of each slice with the softened butter generously. This is important; otherwise, the filling seeps into the bread.

Ham filling: Blend the ham slices to form a paste or mince finely. Mix with parsley and mayonnaise. Refrigerate till needed.

Prawn filling: Mix all the ingredients together. Refrigerate till required.

Pineapple filling: Squeeze the pineapple to get rid of excess moisture. Mix all the remaining ingredients. Refrigerate till needed.

Frosting: Hang the curd in a muslin cloth for a couple of hours to let the whey drain. This hung curd should measure 2 cups. Beat the hung curd with salt, pepper and sugar till smooth. Refrigerate till needed.

To assemble: Place one bread slice, buttered side up on a serving platter. Spread evenly with the ham filling.

Top with the second bread slice. Spread pineapple filling evenly.

Top with the third slice. Spread the prawn filling evenly.

Top with the last bread slice, buttered side down.

Spread the frosting evenly all over the assembled loaf on the top as well as the sides.

Garnish the top with cherries and grapes.

Place in the refrigerator to chill until the frosting is firm, about 1–2 hours. Serve loaf cut into slices.

Serves 4

Note: Sweet chilli sauce is available in the market.

Pinwheel Sandwich

Pretty to look at, equally good to eat.

1 unsliced loaf of bread

Filling: ½ cup butter, softened

$^{1}/_{3}$ cup mayonnaise

¼ cup grated cheese

¼ tsp pepper

¼ tsp salt

¼ cup minced cashewnuts

¼ cup minced dates

¼ cup minced raisins

Trim the crusts of the bread and slice into 5 equal slices lengthwise.

Flatten each slice very lightly with a rolling pin.

Mix all the ingredients for the filling. Spread over the bread slices evenly. Roll up from the narrow ends. Press the ends of the rolls firmly and wrap each roll tightly in butter paper. Refrigerate overnight.

Before serving slice each roll into ¼ thick slices. Arrange on a lettuce lined plate and serve.

Makes 20-25 pinwheels

Note: Instead of this filling, you may also use any other like minced cooked prawns, ham, chicken or grated cheese.

Tivoli Sandwich

A full meal sandwich. Provide knives and forks to eat with.

Italian salad: 1 cup boiled elbow macaroni

1 cup cooked peas

1 cup diced and cooked carrots

½ cup mayonnaise

1 tbsp lime juice

1 tsp sugar

½ tsp salt

pinch of pepper

Fruit salad: 1 small tin pear halves

1 small tin pineapple

2 oranges

1 cup apple, unpeeled and diced

½ cup green grapes

½ cup black grapes

Dressing: 1 cup cream

½ cup sugar

2 tbsp vinegar

¼ tsp salt

You will also need:

4 22-cm French loaves

¼ cup butter, softened

1 bunch lettuce

8 thin slices salami

8 cheese slices halved
24 slices of table radish

Italian salad: Combine mayonnaise, lime juice, sugar, salt and pepper. Stir in the macaroni, peas and carrot. Chill.

Fruit salad: Drain the fruits well and chop into small bits. Peel and divide orange into segments. Peel the membranes and discard the seeds.

Combine all fruits and mix with the dressing. Chill.

To serve: Split each loaf in half lengthwise. Lightly spread the cut sides with butter. Arrange a lettuce leaf on either end of each loaf.

Working from left to right arrange the salami, folded, heaped tablespoon of Italian salad, 2 halved cheese slices folded, 3 radish slices, heaped tablespoon of fruit salad.

Place each sandwich on a plate and place before guests.

Any remaining salad may be served separately.

Serves 8

Open Sandwiches

The open sandwich or 'smorgasbord' was born among the fjords of Scandinavia. They are attractive and good to eat – less bread and more filling. People from other lands fell in love with it and now everybody serves it. These can be sufficiently sustaining for a light meal or small and elegant enough to eat with fingers at a cocktail party.

Use different kinds of bread like brown bread, sandwich bread, French loaf, croissant, buns, etc. Provide knives and forks for guests to eat.

Given below are recipes for two spreads that can be used on the breads.

Cream cheese spread:
This amount is enough for 6–8 slices of bread.
2 cups thick curd
A little milk or cream
¼ tsp salt
½ tsp pepper
pinch chilli powder or 1 small green chilli, finely chopped
1 tbsp finely chopped green coriander
1 tsp sugar or to taste

Tie the curd in a muslin cloth and hang. You'll have solid cream cheese after 2–3 hours. Add a little milk or cream to get a spreading consistency.

Season with salt, pepper, chilli powder and green chilli, fresh coriander and sugar. A few finely chopped nuts of your choice may be added for extra flavour. Mix well. Keep refrigerated till needed.

This also doubles up as an excellent dip that can go with anyt snack.

Eggless Mayonnaise:

½ cup refined oil
6 tbsp milk powder
$^{1}/_{3}$ cup hot water
½ tsp salt
½ tsp mustard powder
A dash of pepper powder
3 tbsp vinegar or lime juice
¼ tsp sugar or to taste

Put the oil, milk powder and water into the blender. Blend at low speed until well mixed.

Add the salt, pepper, mustard powder, vinegar or lime juice and sugar. Blend at high speed till thick and smooth.

Use immediately or store in refrigerator in an airtight container. Refrigeration will preserve it for at least a fortnight.

If you find it too thick, thin down with a little milk or water to the desired consistency.

Makes 1¼ cups

Note: Here are a few ideas for toppings:

1. A cheese slice, topped with two folded slices of ham. Garnish with a twist of orange and a sprig of parsley or fresh coriander.
2. Shredded cabbage or lettuce leaves, topped with sliced cooked chicken and mayonnaise.
3. Slices of salami, laid flat or rolled, topped with sliced boiled egg and chopped gherkin or just raw onion rings. The rolls of salami (or ham) can be filled with potato or mixed vegetable salad or soft cream cheese spread.
4. Luncheon meat slices topped with slices of cucumber, tomato and fresh coriander; or, add potato salad or grated paneer.
5. Slices of paneer topped with eggless mayonnaise, grapes and fresh coriander.

The list is endless; use your imagination and ideas will come to you.

Phalar

This is the standard breakfast in hundreds of Bengali homes during the scorching summer months. It cools the whole body and nourishes you for the day.

1 cup pressed rice
1 large ripe mango
1 large banana
1 cup fresh curd
1 tbsp sugar or to taste
2 cups milk

Wash and soak the pressed rice in 2 cups milk for half an hour.

Peel and dice the mangoes. Press with a fork to crush the pieces roughly. Peel and mash the banana.

Beat the curd and mix with the fruits.

Squeeze the pressed rice gently to get rid of any excess milk.

Add to the curd and mix along with the sugar.

Chill for an hour and serve. Can be served at room temperature also.

Serves 2

Note: Milk may be used in place of curd.

Chicken Chaat

A cross between a snack and a salad; a good way of using up leftover roast chicken.

1 tbsp lime juice
1 tbsp sugar
2 tbsp sweet mango chutney
1 cup mayonnaise
½ tbsp black salt
½ tbsp cumin seeds, roasted and powdered
2 cups chicken, cooked and diced
1 small tart apple
or
1 slice pineapple
1 large potato, boiled and diced
1 small cucumber, peeled and diced
1 small tomato chopped
1 tsp chaat masala
a few lettuce leaves.

Blend the lime juice and sugar with the chutney. Add to it the mayonnaise, black salt and roasted cumin powder.

In a large bowl combine chicken, apple or pineapple, potato, cucumber and tomato. Sprinkle with chaat masala.

Just before serving, mix the chutney—mayonnaise combine to the chicken mix.

Serve on a bed of lettuce leaves.

Serves 4–6

Papri Chaat

This is one of the most popular North-Indian snacks. Papri-Chaat venders are present in almost every roadside. You can very easily make this month-watering snack at home. More hygenic, too!

1 packet ready-made papris
1 cup potatoes, boiled and cut into flakes
¼ cup sprouted moong
¾ cup curd
½ sweet tamarind chutney
½ tsp black salt
¾ cup curd, beaten
½ tsp roasted and powdered cumin
pinch of chilli powder
½ cup sev
a handful of chopped fresh coriander

Divide the papri among 4 serving plates. Top with equal amounts of potatoes and sprouted moong.

Cover with curd and drizzle with chutney. Sprinkle black salt, cumin and chilli powder.

Lastly, top with sev and coriander leaves. Serve immediately.

Serves 4

Misal

This popular low calorie, nutritious Maharashtrian snack can be enjoyed either at breakfast or tea.

1½ cups chirwa (pressed rice)
¾ cup shredded cabbage
¾ cup finely chopped tomato
¾ cup finely chopped onion
¾ cup sprouted moong
¾ cup chopped apple
1½ cups thick curd
4 green chillies, chopped
a handful of chopped fresh coriander
3 tbsp grated coconut
3 bananas sliced
1 tsp salt
2 tsp sugar
½ tsp pepper
½ cup pomegranate seeds for garnishing

Wash and drain the chirwa.
Mix with half the cabbage, tomato, spouted moong, apple, salt and pepper.
Beat the curd and mix with all the remaining ingredients.
Either serve this curd separately or pour over the chiwra placed on a serving dish.

Serves 4

Jhal Muri

This is a Kolkata special. Though it is seen in some other cities also, none can match Kolkata in this amazing snack. All over the city you'll find vendors selling 'Jhal Muri'.

The 'Jhal' or hot part of it comes from the green chillies which you can vary to your taste. But the one essential condiment is fresh mustard oil. No other oil will do.

So, try this quick snack – soon you will get addicted to it!

- 4 cups puffed rice
- 1 small onion, finely chopped
- 2–4 green chillies, finely chopped
- 2 tbsp fresh finely chopped coconut
- ¼ cup roasted gram
- ½ cup boiled and flaked potatoes
- ¼ cucumber, finely chopped
- ½ tsp salt or to taste
- 2 tsp mustard oil

Mix all the ingredients together in a large dry bowl, except the oil.

Finally, add the oil and toss thoroughly so the oil coats all ingredients.

A few drops of lime juice may also be added. Serve immediately.

Goes equally well with hot tea or coffee and cold drinks.

Serves 4

Muesli

Muesli is what is known these days as 'power breakfast'. It became a craze after it was used as part of a health diet in a well-known clinic in Switzerland.

I have altered the ingredients slightly to suit an Indian kitchen. You may change the proportions of the ingredients to your taste.

- 2 cups cornflakes
- 2 cups puffed rice
- 2 cups roasted pressed rice (chiwra)
- 2 cups kheel
- 1 cup mixed roasted nuts
- 2 cups mixed dried fruits (sultanas, apricots, dates, figs, etc.)
- 1 cup raisins

Mix all the ingredients together.

Keep in an airtight container.

Serve 4 tablespoons per portion with milk, curd or fruit juice.

Makes 12 cups

Note: Kheel may be substituted with an equal amount of oats.

Sardine Pate

One of the most elegant ways to start a dinner party is to serve this rich delicious pate.

200 gm can of sardine
4 hardboiled eggs
3 tbsp mayonnaise
1 tbsp Worcestershire sauce
½ cup cream
½ tsp pepper
a few parsley sprigs for garnishing.

Drain the sardines. Cut the tails and remove all bones and scales. Mash flesh with a fork.

Grate the hardboiled eggs with the finest holes of the grater and mix into the sardine with the mayonnaise and Worcestershire sauce. Mix thoroughly.

Whip the cream until thick and fold into the sardine mixture. Add pepper. Taste and adjust seasonings. You may need a dash of salt.

Spoon pate into a serving bowl and smoothen the top. Arrange parsley sprigs in a decorative pattern and chill in the refrigerator until needed.

Serve with hot toasts cut into fancy shapes or savoury biscuits.

Serves 4

Emerald Raita

An Indian meal is incomplete without raita. This pale green delicious raita goes well with any meal.

1 cup hung curd

¼ cup milk or cream

4 tbsp fresh coriander chutney

¼ cup small cubes of paneer

10 green grapes

10 black grapes

1 tbsp grated carrot

Fresh coriander chutney: 2 large bunches fresh coriander

2 green chillies

1 tbsp thick tamarind pulp

1 tsp black salt

1 tbsp powdered sugar

Beat the curd along with the milk or cream. Add the chutney, paneer and halved grapes. Mix well.

Chill and serve, garnished with grated carrot or pomegranate seeds.

Chutney: Take only the leaves of the fresh coriander. Grind with the green chillies and tamarind till smooth. Add salt and sugar. Use as needed. Stays for at least a fortnight if refrigerated.

Serves 4

Note: Any other fruit can be added like pineapple, banana, orange etc.

Sweet and Sour Date Chutney

Fresh ground chutneys are palate-teasing relishes without which any menu tastes bland.

- ½ tsp aniseeds
- 1 tsp cumin seeds
- ½ tbsp coriander seeds
- 1 cup deseeded and chopped dates
- ⅓ cup golden raisins
- 2 tbsp sugar or jaggery
- ¼ cup lime juice
- ½ cup orange juice
- 1 tsp grated ginger
- 2 green chillies, finely chopped
- ¼ tsp salt
- a generous pinch of grated nutmeg
- 2 tbsp chopped fresh coriander
- black salt to taste

Soak the dates and raisins in hot water for 2 hours or longer, if time permits.

Dry roast the aniseeds, cumin seeds and coriander seeds over low heat till they emenate a roasted aroma and turn darker. Remove and grind to a coarse powder.

Drain and blend the dates, raisins, lime juice, orange juice, ginger, green chillies and powdered spices till coarsely ground.

Remove to a bowl. Stir in salt, nutmeg, chopped coriander and black salt.

Can be served immediately. For later use keep it covered tightly. If refrigerated, this will keep for a fortnight at least.

Papaya Fool

A fruit fool is one of the simplest and most delicious of all summer desserts. The main ingredients are just fruit and cream. Custard may be substituted for the cream, but the result is not so good.

1 medium sized papaya, peeled, deseeded and diced
1 cup cream
4 tbsp icing sugar or to taste
grated lime rind for decoration

Blend the papaya to a smooth puree. Whip the cream along with the icing sugar. Fold the whipped cream into the papaya puree.

Spoon the fool into 6 individual bowls and chill for at least 6 hours.

Decorate with grated lime rind and serve with wafers or biscuits.

Serves 6

Note: Any soft fruit can be used the same way. Mango, banana, chickoo, strawberries, custard apple – all make excellent fools.

Lychee Pearls

A most decorative dessert.

16 large lychees
16 whole cashewnuts
16 sheets of silver warq
a pinch of saffron
1 tbsp rose water
1 large tin condensed milk
2 cups milk
½ cup cream
few rose petals for decoration

Peel and deseed the lychees from one side. See to it that the lychees remain whole.

Insert one cashewnut in each lychee in place of the seed. Roll each lychee in silver warq. Keep refrigerated.

Soak saffron in rose water. Beat the condensed milk, milk and saffron till smooth.

Separately whip the cream and gently fold into the condensed milk. Chill.

At the time of serving, top the condensed milk with the lychees. Decorate with rose petals.

Serves 4

Note: 1 cup of grated paneer may be added in place of the cream.

Refrigerator Roll

An excellent, no-cook dessert served with custard or cream. Great as a tea-time snack. Makes good picnic food also.

- 200 gm Marie or thin arrowroot biscuits, ground
- a handful of tutti fruitti or chocolate chips
- ¼ cup white butter
- 1 tin condensed milk
- 2 tbsp dessicated coconut

Mix the biscuit crumbs and tutti fruitti or chocolate chips together. Keep aside.

Beat the butter in a large bowl till fluffy. Add the condensed milk and whip together till mixed well. Add the biscuit crumbs and knead to a dough.

Spread the dessicated coconut over a sheet of butter paper and roll the dough on it to make a large sausage like shape. Wrap the paper well and refrigerate till needed.

Slice and serve with cream or custard, if desired.

Serves 8

Layered Mango Pudding

A wonderful summer treat.

3 medium mangoes
¼ cup castor sugar
finely grated rind and juice of 1 large orange
1½ cups cake crumbs
1 tsp ground cinnamon
To decorate: 4 mango slices
½ cup whipped cream

Peel and dice the mangoes, discarding the seeds.

Blend to obtain 2 cups puree. Strain and mix in the castor sugar.

Mix the grated rind and juice of the orange and cinnamon into the cake crumbs.

Divide half the mango puree into 4 individual glass bowls, then divide half the cake crumbs over the mango puree.

Spoon the remaining mango puree on top and finish with the rest of the crumbs.

Whip the cream until it forms soft peaks and pipe rosettes of cream in the centre of each bowl and decorate with mango slices.

Chill and serve.

Serves 4

Kesaria Shrikhand

A traditional sweet from the western coast of India. In Gujarat, it is invariably served with puris.

- 6 cups fresh curd
- 1 cup sugar, powdered
- 10 tbsp condensed milk
- ½ tsp green cardamom powder
- 10 pistachios, slivered
- 10 almonds, blanched and slivered
- 1 tsp chironji
- pinch of saffron soaked in 1 tbsp milk

Hang the curd in a muslin cloth for 2 hours. Blend the hung curd, sugar or condensed milk and saffron till smooth.

Remove to a serving bowl, adding half the cardamom powder. Mix well. Sprinkle the remaining cardamom powder and nuts on top.

Chill till serving time.

Serves 6–8

Note: You may use 1 tsp rose water instead of the cardamom powder. Shrikhand can also be served topped with fruits.

Chocolate Mousse

For the calorie conscious, this recipe is not just 'naughty', it's plain wicked. But why not? We all deserve a treat every once in a while!

1 cup cream
150 gm cooking chocolate (milk chocolate)
3 eggs, separated
¼ cup powdered sugar
1 tsp vanilla essence
½ cup chocolate chips
½ cup whipped cream for decoration

Break the chocolate in pieces over boiling water. Stir well to remove lumps.

Beat the egg yolk, sugar and vanilla essence till thick and creamy.

Whip the cream to soft peaks. Beat the egg whites until stiff.

Mix the egg yolk mixture with the milked chocolate thoroughly.

Gently fold the cream into the chocolate mix; there should be no streaks of white.

Finally, fold in the egg white and chocolate chips. Mix well.

Spoon into champagne saucers and chill.

Decorate with rosettes of whipped cream and chocolate chips.

Serves 4

Kiltie Cream

Very light and friendly treat!

- ¾ cup cornflakes
- 1 cup cream
- ½ cup hung curd
- 3 tbsp honey or to taste
- 8 strawberries
- 8 cherries

This dessert must be served immediately, otherwise the cornflakes lose their crunch. Chill the cream and curd thoroughly beforehand and prepare the dessert just before serving.

Whip the cream over ice till soft peaks form. Beat the curd till smooth. Fold in the curd, honey and cream with the cornflakes.

Divide the mixture in 4 stem glasses decorated with 2 strawberries and 2 cherries each.

Serves 4

Note: Toasted oats may replace cornflakes. In this case, the dessert may be prepared beforehand and chilled.

Paneer Gateaux

Bound to be a hit in your next high tea party.

- 25 thin arrowroot biscuits
- 6 tbsp soft paneer
- 6 tbsp malai
- 4 tbsp brown sugar
- 4 tbsp finely crushed walnuts.

Beat the paneer, malai and brown sugar together till light and creamy.

Take 5 biscuits per gateaux. Spread a small amount of the paneer mixture over all of them, but one.

Sprinkle a fine layer of the crushed walnuts over the creamed biscuits.

Layer 4 biscuits, one on top of the other. Finish with a plain one.

Wrap each stack of 5 biscuits in aluminium foil tightly. Freeze.

Leave for 24 hours. By this time the biscuits will have softened and become one in texture with the filling.

Serve absolutely chilled.

Makes 5 gateux

Instant Rolls

Unexpected guests will not be a problem if you have the ingredients at hand.

Filling: 2 tbsp chopped multicoloured tutti fruitti
2 tbsp chopped raisins
1 tbsp chopped walnuts
1 tbsp chopped cashewnuts
1 tbsp butter
1 tbsp sugar
Covering: 1 cup powdered sugar or icing sugar
1 cup powdered cashewnuts
¼ tsp vanilla essence
5–6 tsp milk or as need
a pinch of saffron

Filling: Heat the butter and sugar over a low heat till the butter melts. Add the remaining ingredients and remove.
Covering: Mix the milk and saffron. Separately mix together the sugar and cashewnut powder thoroughly. Add the milk and vanilla essence and knead to a pliable dough.
Generously sprinkle a rolling board with icing sugar. Roll the dough to ½ cm thickness.
Spread the filling evenly all over. Roll up carefully from the end nearest to you like a Swiss roll.
Cover with butter paper and chill for an hour. Cut into slices and serve.

Serves 4

Bavarois Diplomate

This striking looking rich souffle makes an excellent dessert for a dinner party. It should be prepared several hours in advance and left to chill. For better visual effect, set in individual champagne saucers or wine goblets.

8 eggs' yolk
2 cups powdered sugar
4 cups cream
7 tbsp strong black coffee
4 tbsp finely chopped, blanched pistachios
few drops of green food colour
6 tbsp finely chopped, blanched almonds
1 tsp vanilla essence
1 tbsp chopped almonds and pistachios for decoration

Put the egg yolk and sugar in a bowl. Place over a pan of hot water and whisk until the mixture reaches the ribbon stage, which means it the whisk is lifted the mixture should fall in a sheet like a ribbon.

Take off the hot water and set the bowl over ice. Whisk continuously until cool.

Whip the cream over ice till thick and fold in the whipped cream lightly with the egg mixture.

Divide the mixture into 3 parts. Flavour one part with the coffee. Take another part, colour it green and add the pistachios. It should be tinted a pale green colour. Mix the third part with the almonds and vanilla essence.

Take a glass dessert bows. Layer the coffee portion. Freeze for 30 minutes. Top with the green portion. Freeze again for half an hour. Finally spread the almond part and freeze till set.

Remove to the lower shelf of the refrigerator till needed.

Unmould onto a plate and serve cut in wedges. Decorate with chopped almonds and pista.

Serves 6

Easy Chocolate Cake

Just the thing for chocoholics.

200 gm Marie or thin arrowroot biscuits, broken into crumbs
2 tbsp chopped walnuts
2 tbsp chopped raisins
4 tbsp chocolate chips
½ cup white butter
1½ tbsp powdered sugar
5 tbsp golden syrup
3 tbsp cocoa powder, sieved
Icing: 1 tbsp unsalted butter
1 tbsp cocoa powder
1 slab (40 gm) milk chocolate
7–8 tbsp icing sugar
2 tbsp hot water

Mix the biscuit crumbs, walnuts, raisins and chocolate chips together. Keep aside.

Beat the butter and sugar together until light and fluffy. Add the golden syrup and beat again. Fold in the cocoa powder. Add the biscuit crumb mixture. Mix well.

Grease a loose bottomed flat tin. Press the crumb mixture well in it. Chill overnight.

Remove the cake from the tin. Pour the icing over it. Chill for 2 hours. Slice and serve.

Icing: Melt the butter and chocolate in a small pan over medium heat.

Add the cocoa powder and remove. Add the sieved icing sugar and hot water. Mix well and use as required.

Serves 8

Note: If you can't get chocolate chips, use a 40 gm bar of chocolate, cut into small pieces.

Paneer Cassata

This recipe won me a prize in a cookery competition.

Curd layer: 3½ cups curd

1/3 cup finely chopped cashewnuts

¾ cup powdered sugar

1 tsp gelatine

1 tbsp cocoa powder

Paneer layer: 1 tsp gelatine

2 cups paneer

1 cup powdered sugar

a few drops of red food colour

1/3 cup multicoloured tutti fruitti.

Sponge cake as needed for lining the mould

whipped cream for decoration (optional)

Line a 20 cm mould with the sponge cake, cutting it to fit the mould. The mould should be lined completely, on the sides also.

Curd layer: Soak the gelatine in 2 tbsp water for 10 minutes. Dissolve over hot water.

Hang the curd tied in a muslin cloth for 2 hours so the whey drains out. Blend with the sugar and cocoa powder so that all are well combined. Mix with the nuts and dissolved gelatine thoroughly.

Pour this mixture over the sponge cake and freeze till set.

In the meantime, proceed with the paneer layer.

Soak the gelatine in 2 tbsp water for 10 minutes. Dissolve over hot water.

Blend the paneer and sugar till smooth. Add a few drops of red colour so that the paneer mixture is tinted a delicate pink.

Add the tutti fruitti and the dissolved gelatine. Mix well.

When the curd mixture is semi set, pour the paneer mixture over it and freeze till firm.

To serve, unmould onto a plate and if desired, decorate with whipped cream.

Serves 6

Vanilla Ice Cream

This ice cream keeps well in the freezer for at least a fortnight.

- 1½ tsp gelatine
- 3 eggs
- ¾ cup sugar, powdered
- 1 tsp vanilla essence
- 2 cups cream

Set your refrigerator at the coldest point before preparing the cream.

Soak the gelatine in 2 tbsp water for 15 minutes; dissolve over hot water keep aside.

Separate 2 eggs into yolk and white. Make sure the white has no specks of yellow and that the bowl is clean and dry.

In a bowl, put 1 whole egg and the 2 egg yolks and whisk till well mixed.

Add the sugar and whisk till light lemon coloured and thick. On this depends the success of your ice cream. Mix the gelatine and vanilla essence.

Beat the cream over ice till thick. Whisk the egg white till stiff, but not dry.

Lightly fold in the cream with the egg yolk mixture. Now, fold in the egg white gently but thoroughly.

Put in an airtight aluminium container. Freeze for one hour. Take out and quickly beat once more. Freeze till set.

Serves 6

Ice Cream Sandesh

This is a most versatile sandesh.

2½ cups fresh homemade paneer, devoid of whey
¾ cup powdered sugar
2 tsp vanilla essence
a pinch of salt

Blend the paneer, sugar, vanilla and salt in the blender till a smooth cream is formed.

Put in an airtight container and freeze. Keep in the lower compartment of refrigerator half an hour prior to serving.

Decorate with chopped nuts and/or tutti fruitti. Cut and serve.

Note: This can also be used as filling for frozen sweet pie. Or else, add 1 tbsp cocoa powder for chocolate sandesh or a pinch of saffron dissolved in 1 tbsp milk for saffron sandesh.

Date and Nut Fingers

200 gm Glucose or Horlicks biscuits
grated rind of 1 lime
1 tbsp lime juice
1 cup chopped nuts of your choice
½ cup deseeded chopped dates
$^{2}/_{3}$ cup condensed milk
icing sugar as needed

Crush the biscuits into fine crumbs. Add the rind and juice of the lime, nuts and dates. Mix well.

Add the condensed milk and bind the mixture well.

Coat a baking tin generously with icing sugar. Put in the mixture. Smoothen the top and sprinkle with icing sugar.

Refrigerate for 2 hours. Cut and serve.

Makes 18–20 fingers